For my grandson Ruairidh—
Happy Second Christmas, with love
– DH

For Jim (Big Mouse) and Raechele (Little Mouse)
– JC

tiger tales
an imprint of ME Media, LLC
202 Old Ridgefield Road, Wilton, CT 06897
Published in the United States 2005
Originally published in Great Britain 2005
By Little Tiger Press
An imprint of Magi Publications
Text copyright © 2005 Diana Hendry
Illustrations copyright © 2005 Jane Chapman
CIP data is available
ISBN 1-58925-051-6
Printed in China

The Very Snowy Christmas

by Diana Hendry

Illustrated by Jane Chapman

tiger tales

It was Christmas Eve.

Big Mouse was making cheese pies. Little Mouse was making paper chains.

"Merry Christmas to us! Merry Christmas to us!" sang Little Mouse. "Big Mouse, can I decorate the Christmas tree now? Can I? Can I?"

"We'll do it together," said Big Mouse.

Little Mouse hung golden acorns and mistletoe berries on the tree.

Big Mouse put a star on the top.

"But we forgot the holly!" cried Little Mouse. "I'll go and get some." And off he ran.

"Make sure it has nice red berries!" called Big Mouse.

MANSION POLISH

Little Mouse set off down the path singing, "Jolly holly! Holly jolly! Jolly holly Christmas!"

But there was no holly to
be seen on the first corner.

And no holly on
the second corner.

And no holly on
the third corner.

So over the bridge ran
Little Mouse...and at last he
found a holly bush with shiny
red berries! He jumped up
and down with excitement.

"Oh jolly holly! Holly jolly! Jolly holly
Christmas!" sang Little Mouse, stretching
high on his toes to reach some.

But suddenly, soft white flakes began falling
all around him. One flake fell on Little Mouse's
nose and made him sneeze. "Goodness me!"
said Little Mouse. "The sky is coming undone!"

As Little Mouse hurried home,
many more pieces of sky fell down
upon him. Faster and faster they
fell. They fell on his ears and his
whiskers and his tail.
"Oh dear, oh dear," said Little Mouse.
"I'd better take some of this home to show
Big Mouse. He'll know how to stitch the sky
together again."

Little Mouse made a ball of
white flakes and put it in his bucket.
Then back over the bridge he hurried.

Suddenly, he saw a strange
creature in the water, making faces
at him! It had lots of ears and a
blurry face, and it waved its arms
at Little Mouse.

"Ooooh! It's a Mouse Ness Monster!"
squeaked Little Mouse, and he fell
on his bottom.

"Oh, I wish Big Mouse was here!"
he cried, scrambling up.

Back down the path ran Little Mouse,
looking over his shoulder to see if the
Mouse Ness Monster was following him.
It wasn't, but something else was!
Little Mouse could see its paw prints
coming after him.

"EEEEkkk! HELP! EEEEkkk!"
squeaked Little Mouse. "Now there's
an Invisible Monster chasing me!"

Little Mouse ran up and down and around and around in circles to escape, but the paw prints of the Invisible Monster went up and down and around and around after him.

Little Mouse ran and ran.
Faster and faster whirled
the white flakes and faster
and faster ran Little Mouse.
And still the Invisible
Monster followed him.

At last, Little Mouse saw his house.
But there in the garden was a huge
White Mouse!
"Oh no, no, no!" squeaked Little
Mouse. "Another monster waiting
to catch me!"
Little Mouse trembled and
began to cry.

But then the front door opened and there was Big Mouse. Little Mouse leapt into Big Mouse's arms.

"Big Mouse, Big Mouse!" he cried. "The sky has come undone! And look!" he wailed, pointing to the paw prints. "An Invisible Monster has been following me, and there was a terrible Mouse Ness Monster in the water, and now that scary White Mouse is staring at me!"

"Oh Little Mouse," said Big Mouse,
"the sky hasn't come undone.
It's SNOWING!

"And there aren't any
monsters. Those are your
paw prints.

"And that Mouse Ness Monster
was your reflection in the water. Look!"
And Big Mouse showed Little Mouse
his face in a puddle.

"And this is a snow mouse I made to welcome you home," he said. "Let's make another." And so they did!

"Snow is magic!" cried Little Mouse.

"Yes," said Big Mouse. "Santa Claus likes snow, too!"

Little Mouse jumped up and down. "Will he be here soon? Can I hang up my stocking now?"

"You can," said Big Mouse. "Let's go and get warm first."

So in they went and warmed their paws by the fire.

Little Mouse hung up his stocking and Big Mouse hung up his stocking, too. The holly berries shone in the firelight.

"It's almost Christmas," said Little Mouse. "Holly jolly, jolly holly Christmas!" And he wiggled his warm toes.